The Hugging Tree

A Story About Resilience

by Jill Neimark

illustrated by Nicole Wong

MAGINATION PRESS
WASHINGTON, DC
American Psychological Association

Published by
MAGINATION PRESS ®
An Educational Publishing Foundation Book
American Psychological Association
750 First Street NE
Washington, DC 20002

Magination Press is a registered trademark of the American Psychological Association.

For more information about our books, including a complete catalog, please write to us, call 1-800-374-2721, or visit our website at www.apa.org/pubs/magination.

Book design by Susan K. White
Printed by Lake Book Manufacturing, Inc., Melrose Park, IL

Library of Congress Cataloging-in-Publication Data
Neimark, Jill, author.
The hugging tree : a story about resilience / by Jill Neimark ; illustrated by Nicole Wong.
pages cm
"An imprint of the American Psychological Association."
 Summary: Told in rhyming text, a little tree clings tenaciously to a granite cliff, determined to live, tended by a little boy, and ultimately loved by the people in the community.
 ISBN 978-1-4338-1907-0 (hardcover) — ISBN 1-4338-1907-4 (hardcover) — ISBN 978-1-4338-1908-7 (pbk.) — ISBN 1-4338-1908-2 (pbk.) 1. Trees—Juvenile fiction. 2. Determination (Personality trait)—Juvenile fiction. 3. Stories in rhyme. [1. Stories in rhyme. 2. Trees—Fiction. 3. Determination (Personality trait)—Fiction.] I. Wong, Nicole (Nicole E.), illustrator. II. Title.
PZ8.3.N338Hu 2015
[E]—dc23   2014036478

Manufactured in the United States of America
First printing May 2015
10 9 8 7 6 5 4 3 2 1

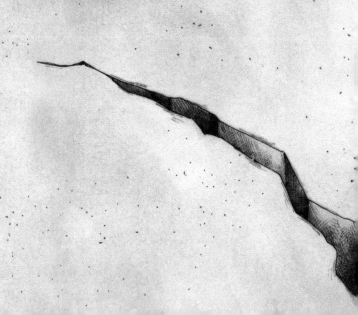

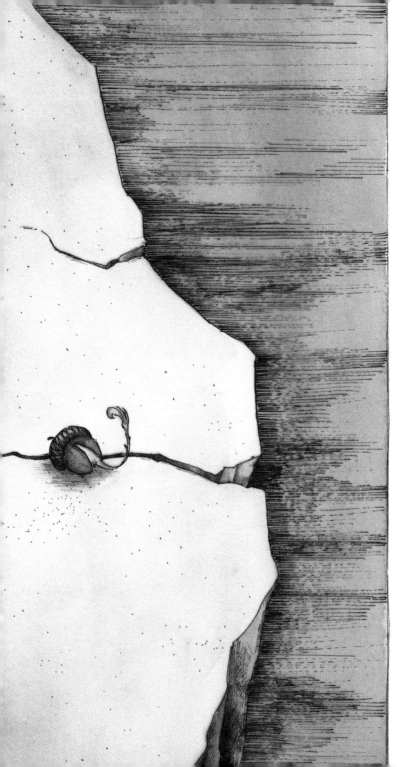

A good half of the art of living is resilience.
—*Alain de Botton*

This has been my vocation, to make music of what remains.
—*Itzhak Perlman*

Ever since Emmy Werner, PhD, conducted her first surprising studies on the resilience of high risk children, researchers have been plumbing the depth and breadth of the remarkable human spirit. Werner followed 700 children for decades, and found that many kids in troubled or abusive homes went on to live healthy and productive lives. Ann S. Masten, PhD, a professor of child psychology at the University of Minnesota–Twin Cities, coined the term "ordinary magic" to explain this mysterious resilience. It is a magic available to us all.

When I first conceived *The Hugging Tree*, I was thinking of my own struggles growing up in a difficult household, and wondering how I personally had come by that little candlelight of hope and resolve in my own life. I thought of trees that grow in unlikely places. How does a seedling prevail, even in rock? How does a tree root as small as a finger slowly displace a few hundred feet of stone? How did the famous "Lone Cypress"—perched precariously on an inhospitable, rocky ocean outcropping in northern California—thrive and become an international tourist attraction?

The title and subject of this book might call to mind the most famous children's book about a tree, *The Giving Tree*, by author and illustrator Shel Silverstein. Certainly the title gives homage to Silverstein's tree. Trees are, and always have been, dear to us. We see in them our protectors. We sense in them the continuity of life. And we find in their steadfastness, our own steadfastness. We marvel at the towering redwoods, the giant sequoias with their immense trunks. Buddhist monks ordain trees, wrapping them in orange robes. Towns name their favorite trees, lovers carve their names in trees, people save trees from being razed to make way for housing projects, and of course, nature lovers are inevitably called "tree huggers."

Trees hold us fast in their embrace. *The Hugging Tree* is about a tree that, in spite of harsh circumstances, grows until it can hold and shelter others. It is about each one of us.

—*Jill Neimark*

On a bleak and lonely rock
by a vast and mighty sea
grew a lonely little tree
where no tree should ever be.

How she got there no one knew.
She sprouted stems and little leaves,
as any tiny seed will do.

"There's hardly any dirt for me.
No forest breeze, no birds, no bees.
But I will do the best I can
to make this rock my home."

Her tiny roots pushed night and day,
and bit by bit the rock gave way.
A smidge, an inch, a foot, then two.
She grew and grew and grew and grew.

The ocean hugged the rocky shore.
"I like you near me, little tree.
Let's keep each other company."

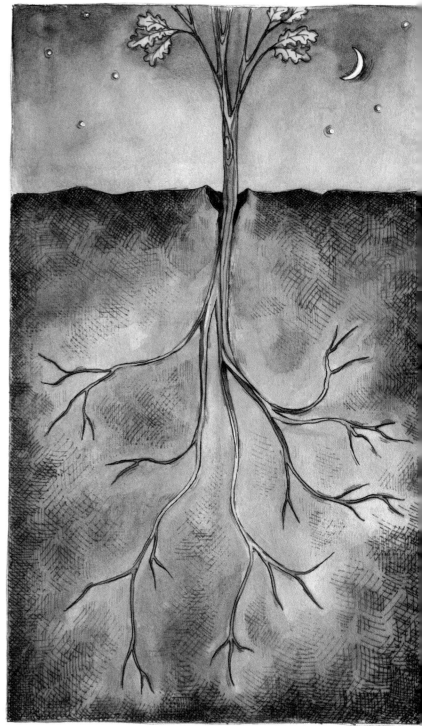

Soft gold sunbeams
kissed her crown,
warm as honey pouring down.

At night she raised her branches high
to greet the moon up in the sky.

"I wax and wane,
I ebb and flow.
I cycle through from full to thin.
And when I'm done,
I start again.
That's how life is, you know."

One summer noon a pair of loons
landed on her canopy.
"A pretty tree, a sparkling sea.
Shall we make this place our home
and raise our baby chicks right here?"

The little tree warmed up with pride.
She spread her branches high and wide.
"I'll be your home," she replied.
"And can you tell me if you've seen
the forest where my family grew?"

"We've built our nest in trees like you
quite far from here, and so you blew
many nights and many days.
You flew on wind just like we do!"

They built their nest, they laid their eggs,
and soon two baby chicks were born.

Summer passed, autumn too.
The little tree turned red and gold.

Then winter came with howling winds
and cutting cold that broke her boughs.

The loons flew south.
The sea all ice,
the rock all snow,
the moon was lost
in thunderclouds.

"Mighty cliff, hold me tight.
Don't let me blow away."

"Little tree, with all my might,
I'll hold you close,
night and day."

Storms will come and storms will go.
At last the sun melted the snow.
But now the tree could not grow.
The storm had torn her roots.

The moon gazed down and softly said,
"Sometimes we lose our way.
But with some help we start again.
That's how life is, you know."

And soon a boy came running by,
skipping stones into the sea.
When he saw the little tree
he stopped and stared.
He touched the tiny leaves.
He felt the ragged roots.
He shook his head and said,

"I can bring just what you need.
I can help you, little tree."

A tree can't hug a boy.
It has no hands or arms.
But it can hug you with its heart,
and that is just as deep and warm.

Every day the boy came back
carrying a full backpack.

From the pack he took a tin
and poured out rich, brown earth.

He packed the roots
and tucked them in.
He planted flowers
round the tree
and made a path for all to see.

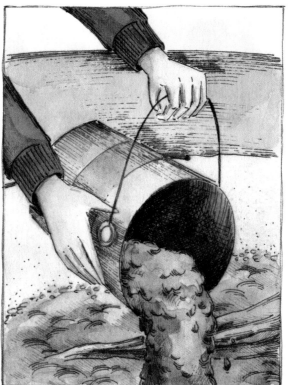

"Now everyone will know
that even on a granite cliff
a little tree can grow."

And then he went to sleep
and dreamed the things
that boys dream of.

Now every day new people stop
to rest beneath the little tree
and dream the things we all dream of.
To love, to share, to give, to dare
to grow just where we are.

And to this very day they come.

For on a splendid sunny rock
by a warm and bright blue sea
a great big hugging tree
grows just where she was meant to be.

Note to Parents and Caregivers

by Elizabeth McCallum, PhD

While we often think of childhood as a wondrous and carefree time, free from the stresses and responsibilities of adulthood, most children face difficulties of various kinds at some point in their formative years. These challenging situations can run the gamut from minor disappointments like losing a sporting event or earning a poor grade on an assignment, to significant emotional traumas stemming from the death of a parent, abuse, or neglect. Psychologists use the term *resilience* to describe an individual's ability to adapt successfully to challenging events. Research has demonstrated that the quality of resilience is associated with numerous long-lasting, positive outcomes, including healthy relationships, self-confidence, and self-control. Although some people seem to be more resilient than others, resilience is not a quality that people are either born with or not—it involves a set of skills that can be learned, encouraged, and nurtured. Parents and caregivers can take steps to encourage this important trait in their children.

HOW THIS BOOK CAN HELP

The Hugging Tree is a peaceful story of caring and compassion that follows the life of a little tree growing all alone on a cliff in harsh environmental conditions. The ocean, moon, and birds are kind to the tree and protect it from the elements, and eventually a young boy brings rich earth to sustain the tree. Throughout the story, the tree withstands challenging conditions and thrives.

Reading this book with your child can be a way to discuss and promote resilience in your child. By discussing the Hugging Tree's resilience amongst the challenging environmental conditions it faces growing all alone on a cliff by the ocean, children

may be encouraged to engage in conversations about the challenges they face at home and at school, and their tools for coping with those challenges.

PROMOTING RESILIENCE IN CHILDREN

All children face some degree of emotional pain and sadness at one time or another. Although parents cannot prevent all childhood fears and anxieties caused by such events, they can teach their children specific strategies and skills for coping with challenging situations. The following are guidelines for building resilience in children.

Help your child connect with others.

Individuals with a wide support system of friends and family are likely to be more resilient because they have others to count on in times of adversity. Help your child build friendships by teaching her

to empathize with others. Kids who are able to express empathy tend to have more and stronger friendships with peers. Simple ways to teach empathy include labeling feelings ("It makes Abby feel sad when you take her favorite toy away") and encouraging your child to think of others ("What do you think your brother would like for his birthday?").

Listen to your children.

Listening to your child's fears or concerns is one of the best ways to encourage resilience. Giving a child your undivided attention communicates that he is important and worthy. Sometimes, finding time to really listen to our children can be difficult when we are balancing all of life's responsibilities. It may be helpful to carve out a few moments per day devoted to each child when he can have your undivided attention to express any thoughts or feelings. During this time, make sure to withhold judgment and simply listen to his concerns. Psychologists use the term active listening to refer to listening and reflecting back someone's concerns ("It sounds like you feel frustrated about the argument you had with your friend"). Actively listening to children makes them feel validated and understood, and often they become better listeners themselves.

Reflect on past successes.
Remind your child of times in the past when she successfully navigated a difficult situation. Discuss the coping strategies she used then and how she could use these or similar strategies when facing current difficulties. Reflecting on past successes can help a child view herself as an individual who has the capacity for success in the face of adversity.

Foster individual strengths.
Help your child set realistic goals and move toward those goals. For instance, if your child is interested in music, encourage him to join the school choir or band. To increase your child's persistence and enjoyment in an activity, provide

praise for both your child's efforts and successes. By gaining competence in a specific area, whether it be academic, athletic, or extracurricular, children gain confidence in their ability to perform in that area. In turn, this confidence can help them persist in the face of future difficulties.

Teach coping skills.
Helping your child cope with stress will give her the tools necessary to face future challenges. You can encourage coping skills by modeling appropriate coping strategies and rewarding your child for appropriate coping techniques. Additionally, when your child uses an ineffective or undesirable coping strategy, such as withdrawing or aggressing, you can help by discussing more adaptive ways of handling the situation. When possible, problem-solve with your child or take steps to

reduce the stressor that is causing your child anxiety. For instance, if your child is worried about an upcoming school test, helping her study will likely be an effective coping strategy to alleviate her stress. In situations in which the stressor cannot be changed (such as parental divorce or the death of a loved one), use strategies to help your child cope with her emotional response to the stressor. Emotion-focused coping techniques include meditation, journaling, and counting to ten before reacting.

Encourage an optimistic viewpoint.
During even the most difficult times, help children take a long-term perspective, encouraging them to remain hopeful that better times are ahead.

Resilience allows children to thrive in the face of the stresses and disappointments of daily life. Encouraging childhood resilience will build skills that children will carry with them into adolescence and adulthood.

Elizabeth McCallum, PhD is an associate professor in the school psychology program at Duquesne University, as well as a Pennsylvania certified school psychologist. She is the author of many scholarly journal articles and book chapters on topics including academic and behavioral interventions for children and adolescents.

About the Author

Jill Neimark is an author of fiction and nonfiction, an award-winning science journalist and essayist, and former features editor at *Psychology Today* magazine. Her credits include the middle-grade novels *The Secret Spiral* and *The Golden Rectangle*, the adult novel *Bloodsong*, which was a Book of the Month Club selection and published in five countries, and the adult nonfiction title *Why Good Things Happen to Good People: How to Live a Longer, Healthier, Happier Life by the Simple Act of Giving* (coauthored with bioethicist Stephen Post, PhD). It was awarded the Kama Prize in Medical Humanities by World Literacy Canada in 2008. This is her third picture book for Magination Press.

About the Illustrator

Nicole Wong is a graduate of the Rhode Island School of Design. Her illustrations have been featured in several children's books, including *No Monkeys, No Chocolate* and *Ferry Tail*. Nicole lives with her husband, daughter, and their dogs and cat in Massachusetts.

About Magination Press

Magination Press is an imprint of the American Psychological Association, the largest scientific and professional organization representing psychologists in the United States and the largest association of psychologists worldwide.